This book is dedicated to my parents
who taught me the importance
of being well-mannered,
and who have always
treated me like a princess.

THIS BOOK BELONGS TO

*the most well-mannered
child in the kingdom*

THE Princess who picked HER NOSE

JILLY REBEIL

Once upon a time there was
a princess named Pearl.
She had big blue eyes
and lovely long curls.

There was practically nothing
the princess couldn't do.
She could read. She could write.
And even tie her shoes.

Princess Pearl was a
perfect ballerina dancer,
and of course she always
had all the answers.

What the young princess had found,
was that her little nose
and fingers were round.
Into her nose her finger would go.
She thought it wouldn't matter–
no one would know.

The king and queen
were clearly distraught.
Princess Pearl picked and picked
even though she knew she should not.

The queen firmly explained,
"Germs come from noses
and picking's quite rude.
Clean hands are important
for manners and food."

Later that night she was snug in her bed,
dreams of ballerinas danced in her head.
The queen insisted on a royal hankie,
but Princess Pearl said,
"I can't blow my nose in this tiny blankie."

Next came the new pair
of little white gloves,
but she threw them in the air
like little white doves.

The nose picking princess
was becoming a very big issue.
The queen just cried and cried
in her pretty little tissue.

Princess Pearl didn't want
her mother to cry.
She picked up a hankie
and gave it a try.

With so many hankies
she could not choose
she just kept blowing and blowing
'til she was almost blue!

could it really be true...?

The kingdom cheered
for what she did not know.
Princess Pearl had just learned
how easy it was to blow.

Even the kitty was proud of Pearl
who learned a lesson
known by every young girl.
Picking your nose is simply not done
by any royal person under the sun!

The next night the king
gave a marvelous feast.
And Pearl was not tempted
to pick in the least.

Hankies and gifts came
from around the world
to celebrate Pearl,
our well-mannered girl!

about THE Author

Inspired by her five children and her love of writing, Jilly Rebeil created a series of books that use love, humor and storytelling to educate children on basic social graces and the importance of being well-behaved. Jilly is married to her own Prince Charming and together they all live "happily ever after" in Laguna Beach, California.